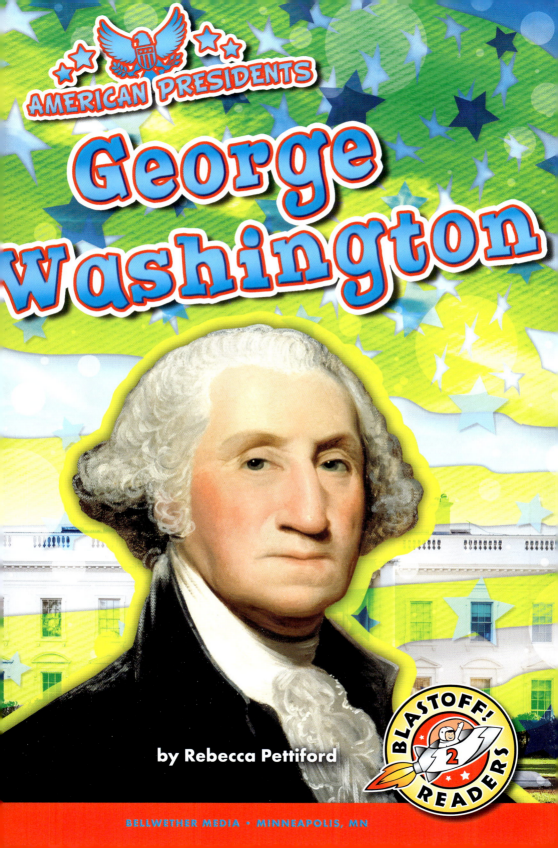

Blastoff! Readers are carefully developed by literacy experts to build reading stamina and move students toward fluency by combining standards-based content with developmentally appropriate text.

Level 1 provides the most support through repetition of high-frequency words, light text, predictable sentence patterns, and strong visual support.

Level 2 offers early readers a bit more challenge through varied sentences, increased text load, and text-supportive special features.

Level 3 advances early-fluent readers toward fluency through increased text load, less reliance on photos, advancing concepts, longer sentences, and more complex special features.

★ **Blastoff! Universe**

Reading Level

Grade K

Grades 1–3

Grade 4

This edition first published in 2022 by Bellwether Media, Inc.

No part of this publication may be reproduced in whole or in part without written permission of the publisher. For information regarding permission, write to Bellwether Media, Inc., Attention: Permissions Department, 6012 Blue Circle Drive, Minnetonka, MN 55343.

Library of Congress Cataloging-in-Publication Data

Names: Pettiford, Rebecca, author.
Title: George Washington / by Rebecca Pettiford.
Description: Minneapolis, MN : Bellwether Media, Inc., 2022. | Series: Blastoff! Readers: American Presidents | Includes bibliographical references and index. | Audience: Ages 5-8 | Audience: Grades 2-3 | Summary: "Relevant images match informative text in this introduction to George Washington. Intended for students in kindergarten through third grade"-- Provided by publisher.
Identifiers: LCCN 2021011391 (print) | LCCN 2021011392 (ebook) | ISBN 9781644875155 (library binding) | ISBN 9781648344831 (paperback) | ISBN 9781648344237 (ebook)
Subjects: LCSH: Washington, George, 1732-1799--Juvenile literature. | Presidents--United States--Biography--Juvenile literature.
Classification: LCC E312.66 .P48 2022 (print) | LCC E312.66 (ebook) | DDC 973.4/1092 [B]--dc23
LC record available at https://lccn.loc.gov/2021011391
LC ebook record available at https://lccn.loc.gov/2021011392

Text copyright © 2022 by Bellwether Media, Inc. BLASTOFF! READERS and associated logos are trademarks and/or registered trademarks of Bellwether Media, Inc.

Editor: Elizabeth Neuenfeldt   Designer: Josh Brink

Printed in the United States of America, North Mankato, MN.

Table of Contents

Who Was George Washington?	4
Time in Office	12
What George Left Behind	20
Glossary	22
To Learn More	23
Index	24

Who Was George Washington?

George Washington was the first president of the United States. George was one of the **founding fathers**!

He served from 1789 to 1797.

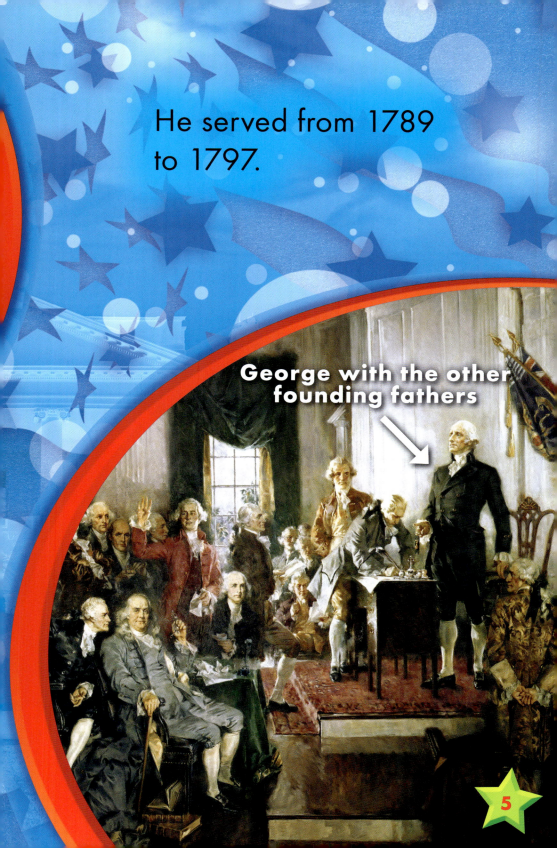

George with the other founding fathers

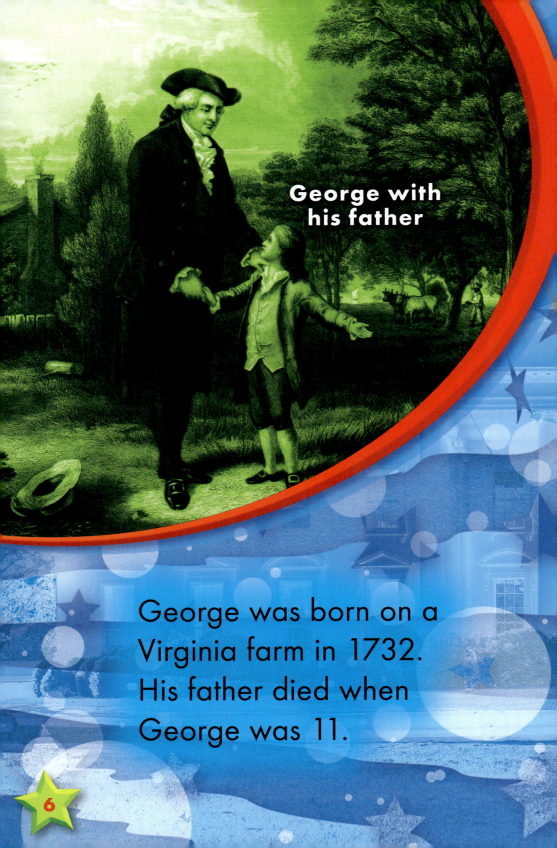

George with his father

George was born on a Virginia farm in 1732. His father died when George was 11.

George learned with **tutors**. In 1749, he became a **surveyor**.

Presidential Picks

Animals

dogs and horses

Hobbies

dancing and reading

Sport

fox hunting

Food

hoecakes

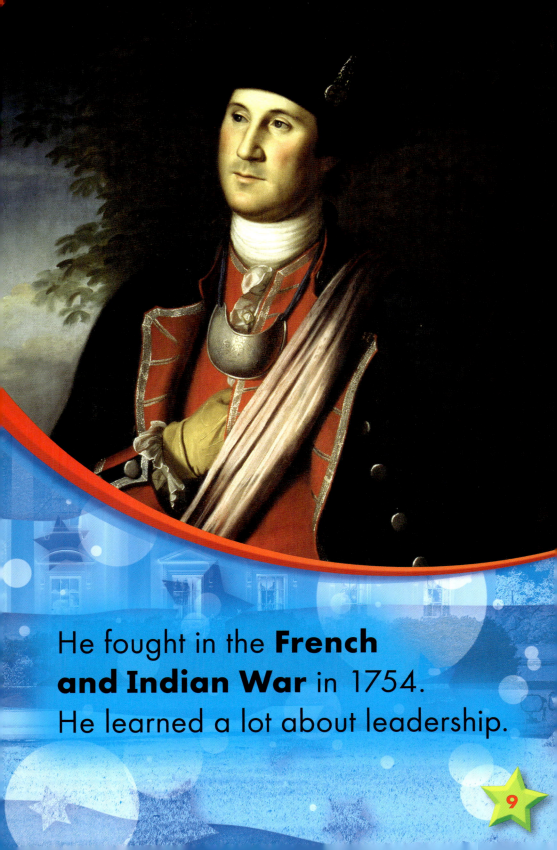

He fought in the **French and Indian War** in 1754. He learned a lot about leadership.

In 1758, George began working in the Virginia government.

The **Revolutionary War** began in 1775. George led the army. He helped the U.S. win!

Question

What helped George become a stronger leader?

George in the Revolutionary War

Time in Office

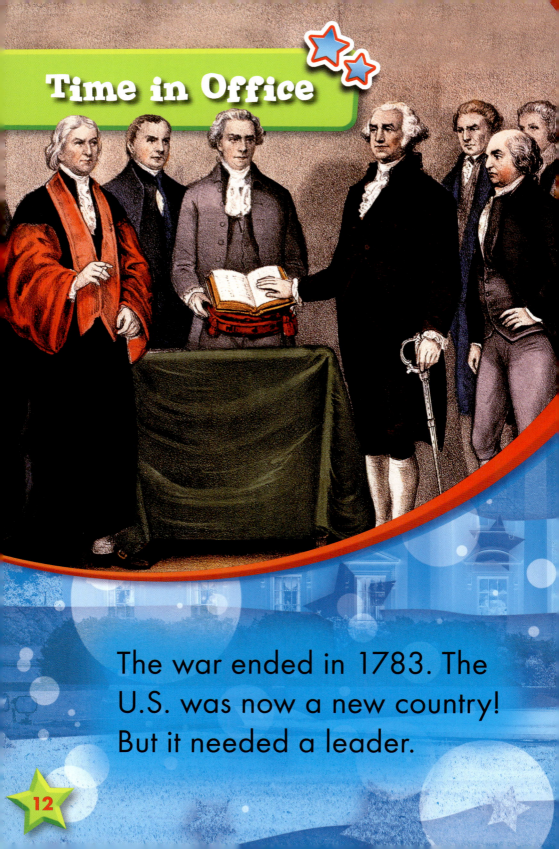

The war ended in 1783. The U.S. was now a new country! But it needed a leader.

In 1789, George was **elected** president.

Presidential Profile

Place of Birth

Pope's Creek, Virginia

Birthday

February 22, 1732

Schooling

tutors

Term

1789 to 1797

Party

none

Signature

Vice President

John Adams

In 1790, George chose the location of the U.S. **capital** city. It is now called Washington, D.C.!

U.S. Capitol Building

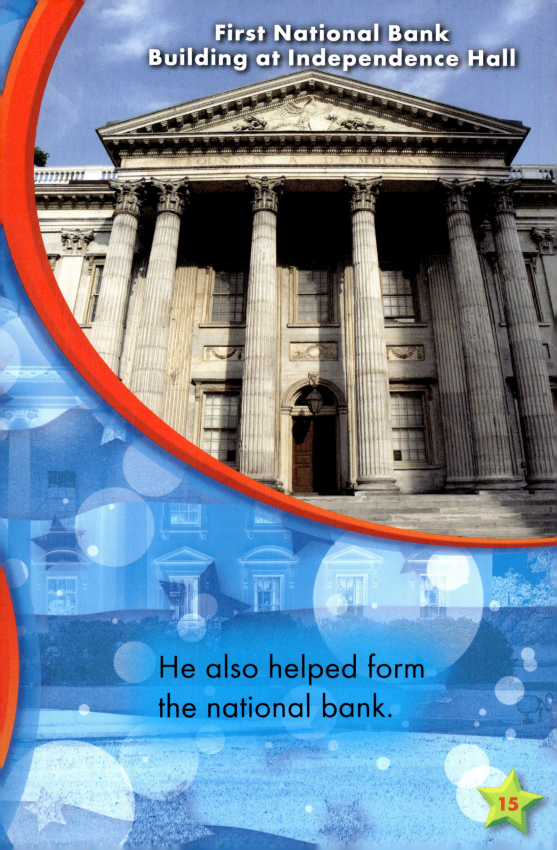

First National Bank Building at Independence Hall

He also helped form the national bank.

In 1791, the **Bill of Rights** was signed. It helped give people rights.

George was reelected in 1792. He won by many votes!

Bill of Rights of 1791

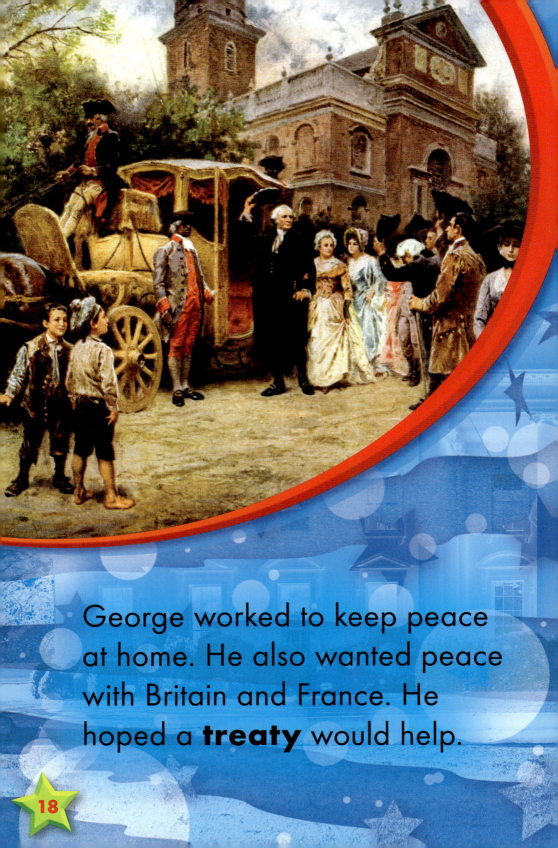

George worked to keep peace at home. He also wanted peace with Britain and France. He hoped a **treaty** would help.

George Timeline

February 4, 1789
George Washington is elected the first U.S. president

February 25, 1791
George helps form the national bank

December 15, 1791
The Bill of Rights is signed

December 1792
George is reelected

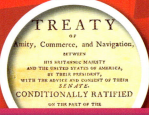

August 1795
George signs the Jay Treaty

March 4, 1797
George leaves office

What George Left Behind

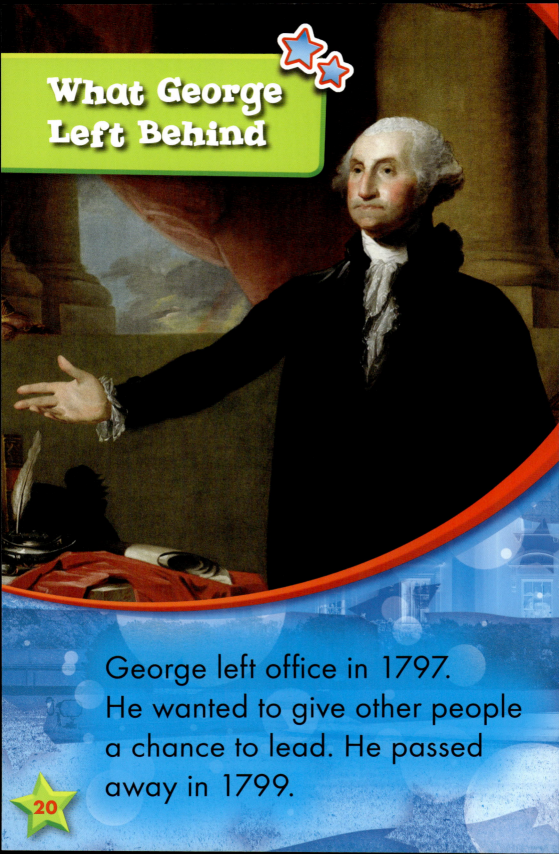

George left office in 1797. He wanted to give other people a chance to lead. He passed away in 1799.

His leadership helped create the U.S.!

Washington Monument

Glossary

Bill of Rights—a written statement that lists the basic rights of residents in the U.S.; rights are things that people should be allowed to have, get, or do.

capital—a city that houses the main offices of a government

elected—chosen by voting

founding fathers—the men who helped create the government of the United States

French and Indian War—a war between Britain and France over land in North America that was part of a larger war between Britain and France called the Seven Years' War

Revolutionary War—the war from 1775 to 1783 in which the United States fought for independence from Britain

surveyor—someone who measures and studies land

treaty—an agreement made between two or more countries or groups

tutors—teachers who work with a single student

To Learn More

AT THE LIBRARY
Hally, Ashleigh. *George Washington*. New York, N.Y.: AV2 by Weigl, 2018.

Murray, Laura K. *George Washington*. North Mankato, Minn.: Capstone, 2020.

Ransom, Candice. *George Washington*. Minneapolis, Minn.: Pop!, 2019.

ON THE WEB

FACTSURFER

Factsurfer.com gives you a safe, fun way to find more information.

1. Go to www.factsurfer.com.

2. Enter "George Washington" into the search box and click 🔍.

3. Select your book cover to see a list of related content.

Index

army, 10
Bill of Rights, 16
Britain, 18
capital, 14
elected, 13, 16, 17
farm, 6, 7
father, 6
founding fathers, 4, 5
France, 18
French and Indian War, 9
hometown, 7
leadership, 9, 12, 20, 21
national bank, 15
picks, 8
peace, 18
profile, 13
question, 11
Revolutionary War, 10, 11, 12
surveyor, 8
timeline, 19
treaty, 18
tutors, 8
Virginia, 6, 7, 10
votes, 16
Washington, D.C., 14

The images in this book are reproduced through the courtesy of: ICP/ Alamy, cover; Jorge Salcedo, p. 3; Metropolitan Museum of Art, online collection/ Wikimedia Commons, p. 4; The Indian Reporter/ Wikimedia Commons, p. 5; Archive Images/ Alamy, p. 6; TanyaCPhotography, p. 8 (dog); Dudarev Mikhail, p. 8 (reading); NEIL ROY JOHNSON, p. 8 (fox hunting); Glenn Price, p. 8 (hoecakes); The Picture Art Collection/ Alamy, p. 9; North Wind Picture Archives/ Alamy, p. 10; IanDagnall Computing/ Alamy, p. 11; JT Vintage/ Alamy, pp. 12, 16-17; George Washington, Raeky/ Wikimedia Commons, p. 13 (signature); White House Research/ Wikimedia Commons, p. 13 (John Adams); Orhan Cam, p. 14; trekandshoot, p. 15; Science History Images/ Alamy, p. 18; Jose Luis Stephens, p. 19 (national bank); Everett Collection, p. 19 (reelection); Early America/ Wikimedia Commons, p. 19 (Jay's Treaty); Artepics/ Alamy, p. 20; Bitkiz, p. 21; Kovalchuk Oleksandr, p. 23.